SHEEP ASLEEP

SHEEP ASLEEP

by Gloria Rothstein

illustrated by Lizzy Rockwell

HARPERCOLLINS*PUBLISHERS*

10 sheep almost

"Put on your

ready for bed—

pajamas," Mama said.

"Try to brush

teeth and faces—

between the spaces."

8 sheep making

"Please put away

too much noise—

ALL your toys."

7 sheep acting

"Close the window.

very silly—

It's getting chilly."

6 sheep piling

"You can reach.

up dirty clothes—

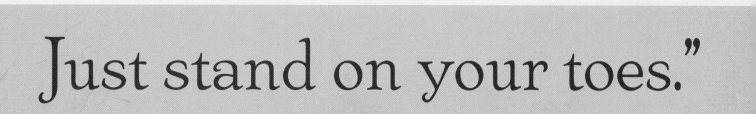

Just stand on your toes."

5 sheep jumping

five

"Not so high.

on the bed—

You'll bump your head."

4 sheep sharing
four

"Let your brother

a bedtime book—

PIGS' BIG GAME

MA · PIGS' BIG GAME · PORKY PRESS

by KAREN MA

take a look."

3 sheep still

three

"Tomorrow is

determined to play—

another day."

2 sheep having
two

"Didn't I already

a pillow fight—

say good night?"

1 sheep
one

"I think it's time

still can't fall asleep—

for counting sheep."

1...2...3...

4...5...6...

9…

sheep

asleep!

For my sons, Ryan and Hale, who always
count on their mom's little reminders!
—with love, G. R.

To Nigel
—L. R.

Sheep Asleep
Text copyright © 2003 by Gloria Rothstein
Illustrations copyright © 2003 by Lizzy Rockwell
Manufactured in China. All rights reserved.
www.harperchildrens.com

Library of Congress Cataloging-in-Publication Data
Rothstein, Gloria.
  Sheep asleep / by Gloria Rothstein ; illustrated by Lizzy Rockwell.
    p.   cm.
  Summary: Ten sheep who don't want to go to sleep have fun counting down to bedtime.
  ISBN 0-06-029105-2 — ISBN 0-06-029106-0 (lib. bdg.)
  [1. Counting.   2. Bedtime—Fiction.   3. Sheep—Fiction   4. Stories in rhyme.]
I. Rockwell, Lizzy, ill.   II. Title.

PZ8.3.R753 Sh   2003   00-049878
[E]—dc21   CIP
                                                                              AC

Typography by Elynn Cohen 1 2 3 4 5 6 7 8 9 10 ❖ First Edition